Copyright © 1988 Nord-Süd Verlag, Mönchaltorf, Switzerland
First published in Switzerland under the title Lieber Schneemann,
wohin willst du?
English text copyright © 1988 Rosemary Lanning
Copyright English language edition under the imprint
North-South Books © 1988 Rada Matija AG, 8625 Gossau ZH, Switzerland

First published in the United States, Great Britain, Canada,
Australia and New Zealand in 1988 by North-South Books,
an imprint of Rada Matija AG.

Printed in Italy

Library of Congress Catalog Card Number: 88-42532

British Library Cataloguing in Publication Data

Scheidl, Gerda Marie
Flowers for the Snowman.
I. Title II. Wilkoń, Józef III. Lieber
Schneemann, wohin willst du? *English*
833'.914[J]

ISBN 3-85539-002-9

Flowers for the Snowman

Gerda Marie Scheidl
Illustrated by Józef Wilkoń

Translated by Rosemary Lanning

North-South Books

In the middle of an open field stood a snowman. He had a long carrot nose and was wearing a big, floppy hat.

There he stood, looking thoroughly miserable. Why? Because wherever he turned his coal black eyes, all he could see was snow. The snowman was very disappointed. He had imagined the world to be quite different – not white, but full of color. He had heard that there were flowers here. Flowers in all the colors of the rainbow. But where were they?

The snowman thought deeply about this. "Something's not right," he said, "but what is it?" He wrinkled his carrot nose. "I've got it!" he exclaimed. "I'm in the wrong place. The flowers must be somewhere else."

The next morning the snowman set off to find the colorful flowers. On his way he met a hare nibbling a cabbage stalk.

"Is that a flower?" asked the snowman politely.

"A flower?" The hare somersaulted with surprise. "Of course not. It's a cabbage stalk."

"Not a flower. What a pity. Where *will* I find flowers, flowers in all the colors of the rainbow?"

Snowman dear, it's sad I know,
but since you're only made of snow
you'll never see the flowers grow,

mumbled the hare, and he hopped away.

"Bah!" snorted the snowman. "Why shouldn't I ever see flowers, just because I'm made of snow?"

The snowman plodded on until he came to a forest. All the trees were cloaked in a thick layer of snow. Only one small tree was showing its usual coat of green needles. It was crouching under the protective branches of a bigger pine tree.

"Is this a flower?" the snowman asked a passing crow.

"Silly!" croaked the crow. "That's not a flower. It's a pine tree."

"Oh," said the snowman doubtfully. "Where will I find flowers, then? Really colorful flowers."

Snowman dear, it's sad I know,
but since you're only made of snow
you'll never see the flowers grow,

cawed the crow, and it flew away.

"Silly, am I?" muttered the snowman. "It's the crow who's silly. I *am* going to see flowers, flowers in all the colors of the rainbow."

And he plodded on again. It was night time when he came to a town.

"Hello! Is there anyone there?" he called as he wandered through the dark streets. "Hello!" he called again. But no one answered. Everyone was asleep. "There must be flowers in a town," thought the snowman. But try as he might, he couldn't find flowers anywhere. Or could he?

"Is this a flower?" he asked a cat who was sitting on a street
lamp. The lamp was painted green, and its light glittered
brightly. It looked so pretty.

"Meow! No! This isn't a flower. It's an ordinary street
lamp!" retorted the cat.

"What a shame. But where can I find flowers, really
colorful flowers?"

Snowman dear, it's sad I know,
but since you're only made of snow
you'll never see the flowers grow,

mewed the cat, and it scampered away.

Would he really never see any flowers? Just because he was made of snow? The snowman felt so sad, and tired too. He trudged across a courtyard.

"Aah, I can rest here for a while," he yawned, and leant against a door.

The snowman shouldn't have done that. The door gave way
and he tumbled head over heels down a flight of stairs. Oh
dear! Where had he landed now? The snowman looked
anxiously around. And what do you think he saw? Oh! How
lovely! He'd never seen anything like it before. Could these
be flowers?

"Are you … are you … flowers?" he stuttered.

"Yes, we're flowers," came a whisper from all sides.

Of course they were flowers. The snowman had stumbled
into the greenhouse at a garden center. It was lovely and
warm in there, to protect the flowers from the frost.

"At last I've found some flowers!" cried
the snowman. "Flowers in all the colors
of the rainbow!" He had never felt so
happy as he did just then.

"They make my heart glow with joy,
but oh, I feel so weak," he sighed
wearily, shutting his coal black eyes.

He slipped into a dream. And what do
you think he dreamt about?
      He dreamt he was standing in a
green meadow, among many colored
flowers. He bent down and picked a big
bunch of them.

Then he sat on the grass,
and then ... his dream came to an end.

"Well I never!" said the head gardener the next morning. "This looks as if it was once a snowman. Out you go! This is no place for someone made of snow." And he shoveled what was left of the snowman into the yard.

Snowman dear, it's sad I know,
but you were only made of snow ...

and because you were made of snow, you shouldn't have

gone looking for flowers. This was bound to happen. Now you're just a small heap of melting snow.

"Poor snowman!" cried the children. "Let's make a new one."
    And they gathered the little heap of snow into a ball, then made another and another. They rolled the three snowballs through the snow to make them bigger and bigger.

Then the children piled the three snowballs on top of one another. They stuck snow arms on each side. Then they added a carrot nose and coal black eyes, and put the big floppy hat on his head.

Hooray! They had finished.

And the new snowman didn't look miserable at all.

He was smiling, for he was thinking about flowers, flowers in all the colors of the rainbow.